Grasses of a Thousand Colors

Grasses of a Thousand Colors

Wallace Shawn

REVISED EDITION

THEATRE COMMUNICATIONS GROUP
NEW YORK
2014

The publication of *Grasses of a Thousand Colors*, by Wallace Shawn, through TCG's Book Program, is made possible in part by the New York State Council on the Arts with the support of Governor Andrew Cuomo and the New York State Legislature.

TCG books are exclusively distributed to the book trade by Consortium Book Sales and Distribution.

LIBRARY OF CONGRESS CATALOGING-IN-PUBLICATION DATA
Shawn, Wallace.
Grasses of a thousand colors / Wallace Shawn.—Revised Edition.
pages cm
Originally published by New York, Theatre Communications Group, 2009.
ISBN 978-1-55936-478-2 (pbk.) ISBN 978-1-55936-790-5 (ebook)
1. Scientists—Drama. 2. Cats—Drama. 3. American drama. I. Title.
PS3569.H387G73   2014
812'.54—dc23   2013046537

Cover design by Mark Melnick
Front cover photograph: *Entrance* (2008), Bryan Graf
Back cover image: Mainzer Card Company
Text design and composition by Lisa Govan

First Edition, April 2009
Revised Edition, February 2014

To some people, folk tales, fairy tales, and myths seem like the most realistic narratives. Did my father enchant Mr. Behrman to write that book—in order to lead me to you? When I was a boy, did Behrman enchant me, with his conjurer's tales about the theater, plays, actors, costumes, to send me to André, Gerry, Cecil—you? Was Marvin real? And were the false dimes in subway telephone booths, the parties, the friends, all merely tricks and enchantments whose true purpose was to lure you out and bring you to me?

I would have slept through everything. If you had just walked by, if you hadn't stopped—

For darling D, from W

Grasses of a
Thousand Colors

Grasses of a Thousand Colors received its world premiere on May 18, 2009, at the Royal Court Theatre, London. The production was directed by André Gregory, with design by Eugene Lee, costumes by Dona Granata, lighting by Howard Harrison, sound by Bruce Odland and video by Bill Morrison. The stage manager was Catherine Buffrey. The cast was:

THE MEMOIRIST (Ben)	Wallace Shawn
CERISE	Miranda Richardson
ROBIN	Jennifer Tilly
ROSE	Emily Cass McDonnell

Grasses of a Thousand Colors had its New York premiere in a co-production by The Public Theater (Oskar Eustis, Artistic Director; Patrick Willingham, Executive Director) and Theatre for a New Audience (Jeffrey Horowitz, Artistic Director; Dorothy Ryan, Managing Director) on October 28, 2013. The production was directed by André Gregory, with design by Eugene Lee, costumes by Dona Granata, lighting by Howard Harrison, sound by Bruce Odland, video by Bill Morrison and special assistance by Rob Weiner. The production stage manager was Jennifer Rae Moore. The cast was:

THE MEMOIRIST (Ben)	Wallace Shawn
CERISE	Julie Hagerty
ROBIN	Jennifer Tilly
ROSE	Emily Cass McDonnell

On October 9, 15, 23, 30, and November 5, 14, 23, 27, the part of Robin was played by Emily Cass McDonnell and the part of Rose was played by Kristina Mueller.

Characters

THE MEMOIRIST (Ben), over sixty-five
CERISE, younger than Ben
ROBIN, younger than Ben
ROSE, younger than the others

Part One

A lectern. A waste basket. A sofa.

HE

Well. Hello, everybody! Hello! Hello there! Ha ha ha. You know, it's so wonderful that you've come to see me here this evening. I mean, I know you're busy, and you're probably just as mixed up as I am. Because things have obviously changed since yesterday, that's totally clear, things are definitely different, in one way or another. Well, it's been quite a journey—my God. The last part of it was crazy! And I know you could have signed up for any of a million things tonight, but anyway, you chose to come listen to me, and here we all are. Now, did they give you any of this? *(He takes out a small bottle with a brightly colored liquid in it)* Because I said, "Oo, I'm feeling a bit weak, or a bit giddy or something," and somebody just handed me one of these and said, "Look, if you feel like *that*, take some of *this*"—well, I don't know if I'm going to try it . . . *(He goes to the lectern and sets the bottle on it next to an empty glass)* Anyway, I'm *so* excited that you've come to hear me talk about myself tonight, and I'm very eager to tell you all about my life, but I have to admit that I've been having terrible memory problems recently, and I must say the last few years are a complete blank, I seriously don't remember them at all. I don't even remember yesterday. I can't remember anything about it. I don't even remember where I *was*, much less what I did. *(He pauses)* But luckily for me *and* you, several years ago I actually wrote my memoirs, *(He points to a huge book on the lectern)* and so what I'm going to do tonight is to read you some sections from this rather fascinating book. And I don't know quite what I ought to say by way of introduction, but one thing I certainly *will* say is that I love this room—isn't it great?— in fact, I've just decided to give this room a name. I'm going to call this room "the satin heart," because it sort of looks like that, you see, it sort of looks like a chocolate box, in a certain sense, and of course, to me, all of you have just become chocolates in a way, because when you're all so nicely sitting there and listening to me, I'm deriving a great deal of pleasure from each and every one of you, as if you were chocolates I was eating—ha ha ha!—and some of you are sort of whiskey-flavored, and some are sort of coffee-flavored, or whatever, but I can taste each one of you distinctly, and it's a delicious experience. And of course I know I'm greeting you a bit informally here in my dressing gown and slippers, but everything has always felt so much nicer to me whenever I've been able to be comfortable with the clothes I'm wearing, and I've always hated the very tight, constricting clothes that men have always traditionally worn. *(He stops for a moment)* You know, I feel so weak,

I think I'm just going to try some of this. *(He opens the bottle, pours some of the liquid into the glass, and drinks. He perks up)* Hm, not bad. Actually quite good! Oh yes, that feels much better.

So now I definitely want to tell you about what happened yesterday. Because you see, it was exactly eight o'clock yesterday morning when I finally sat down to my breakfast table. And my breakfast table, you see, is outside, on my balcony, on a sort of golden terrace looking out on the sea, and so it's all quite lovely, but what I was of course obliged to do there, as at every meal, was to somehow manage to swallow a few spoonfuls of the gritty, thin, horrible gruel that I was most unfortunately obliged to eat. I'm sure that almost all of you know all too well what I'm talking about. Now, in the place where I lived, the impresario of gruel happened to be Dr. Felix Gross. Have you heard of him? Well, he was our Nutritionist to the Privileged, and so it was his very demanding job to keep all of his patients very well supplied with these different weekly batches of disgusting gruel which more or less kept up week by week with the ever-changing slippery development of the awful stomach illness which so suddenly and so mysteriously had changed the lives of so many humans on earth. Well, if there's anyone here who's come from a very remote area and who perhaps requires a brief analysis of that—you know, what can I say? To be rather simple about it— Well, everyone knows that a human being can't keep itself going—can't create energy, strength, or warmth for itself or keep itself alive—by swallowing a mouthful of stones. But it also can't keep itself going or keep itself alive by swallowing a mouthful of rice, unless and until that rice has been chemically transformed inside its body into a substance that's able to perform those functions. Digestion, in other words, is a wonderful and complicated process, and it can obviously fail or fall apart at any one of its thousands of wonderful and complicated junctures, and, for whatever mysterious reason, there came a moment when most of us simply couldn't digest most foods anymore, and the list of foods we *could* digest kept changing and ultimately shrinking, as more and more foods became impossible for each of us to eat. Most people started living off this government-processed gruel that almost always fell behind, so that for most people the excruciating stomach pain and the vomiting and the other expressions of digestive collapse got worse and worse as each day wore on, so that by evening they were subsisting in a kind of agony. And so, in the place I lived, well, Gross's gruel was a more effective type of gruel, or so we hoped, or so we always said, and according to certain statistics we lived much longer than the less privileged people, or at any rate we all devoutly *believed* we did, whether it was true or not. In any case, even with Gross's help, we woke up in pain every day, with our stomachs terribly sore and sort of throbbing, and if we were lucky we would have managed three or four hours of sleep, perhaps interrupted only once or twice by a brief, quickly dispatched vomit or two. And it was in that condition that all of us set about eating our so-called breakfasts each day—in my case, certainly, after recalling for a moment the marmalade, butter, coffee, cream, rolls, toast, and boiled eggs that I used to be able to eat. So, at any rate, yesterday, I hadn't had more than two spoonfuls of gruel when quite unexpectedly the young woman I lived with—Rose—suddenly appeared on my balcony holding a letter addressed to me that had just been delivered to our door. Now Rose was extremely close to my wife, Cerise, and Rose quite often received letters from Cerise, because Cerise lived quite far away, way off in the country. But it had been a very long time since anyone had written a letter to me. So Rose gave me the letter and walked away without saying very much, and I opened the envelope, and it seemed to be an invitation of some kind— and then suddenly I sneezed. Cat dander? That seemed odd. And the invitation, rudely, was for that very afternoon, and it was signed simply, "Love, Blanche." Well, that was odd, too, because Blanche—the only Blanche *I* knew—was certainly dead. I knew she was dead, because I'd been present at her death. And the other thing that was odd was that the Blanche I knew was definitely a cat, and even if they're very much alive, cats can't write. Well, so there was something curious, clearly, but I thought to myself, Well, I mean, of course I'll *go*. I mean, you know, why wouldn't I? . . .

But, at any rate, to get back to my memoir, please let me start by reciting for you the epigraph I chose for it after a certain amount of thought. It's by Count D'Aurore, and it goes like this: "When I finally awakened after a long, long sleep with many dreams, I was surprised to find that I was lying on a battlefield and holding a sword. It was just after dawn, the air was cold, and the ground was damp with my own blood. As I wondered what circumstances could have brought me here, I looked across the vast expanse of the plain on which I lay, and it seemed that I could see grasses of a thousand colors, in which many rabbits, in absolute silence, were leaping and running like small horses." And now let me read you the very beginning of my book. *(And now he reads)* "I'm a lucky person. I was born lucky. And to call a person 'lucky' means, really, that good things sort of rush towards that person, sort of fly towards them somehow, special privileges that other people don't have, and the privileges sort of carve out little channels in the fabric of the universe, channels that flow in that person's direction, so that each good thing that went in their direction yesterday helps to make it more likely that more good things will go in their direction today. And I'm a lucky person. And it's nice to be lucky, because other people can't help being drawn to people who are lucky—it's part of our fundamental makeup—and even words like 'friendship' and 'love' mainly refer to the feelings that draw us all towards lucky people, and so lucky people are always surrounded by friends and get to pick whoever they like to keep them company every day, which is a very agreeable situation."

(He looks up from the book and speaks to the audience) And at a certain point in the book I explain why I was never one of those people who complained about their luck, why I was never one of those people who felt guilty because they were lucky. And I explain why I think there's a certain idiocy in that sort of complaining. *(And now he reads)* "I came, you see, from an optimistic generation. Everyone I knew from my generation was a fixer, an improver. We were born that way, apparently. We loved to solve problems. Was someone dissatisfied with how fast he could run? Was someone dissatisfied with how fast he could think? We saw these as problems that *could be solved*. But of course the one thing that in principle *cannot* be solved is luck. You can't fix luck. There's good luck for some people and bad luck for other people—and that's just the way things work in the universe that human beings live in—that's the way they *have* to work, because, in that particular universe, in regard to whatever's bigger than an atom, each thing has a certain location, and no two things can share exactly

the same location. If one person is situated in a particular place, right in the middle of this sofa, let's say, then no other person can occupy that place. And so in any line of ducks in a pond, one duck and only one duck can be in front, and one duck and only one duck will be in back. Only one face of the dice can stand on top—not all six. And in the game of 'musical chairs,' the number of chairs is always one less than the number of people, and when the music stops, there's always one person who has no chair."

(He looks up from the book and speaks to the audience) So I explain that I began my life in fortunate circumstances. And in the first chapter I explain how I grew up, how I became a doctor, and everything about my early life. And the second chapter begins with that fateful night at the Grand Circle restaurant, when five other young doctors and I passed around six of that restaurant's blue paper napkins, and we each wrote down on our napkin our answer to the question: "What is the greatest problem facing the world today?" And incredibly we all came up with essentially the same answer. Because we could all see, on the one hand, an enormous crowd of entities, ourselves and others, who were roaming the planet trying to sustain themselves, looking for something to eat—but on the other hand, we could see only a tiny, inadequate crowd of entities who were sitting there on the planet, waiting and available to *be eaten*. So in other words, there was a problem about food. It was all about food. There wasn't enough food. And after we left the restaurant, I went home, and I stayed up all night, and the next morning, I went to my office and told my secretary that I was going to wind down my private medical practice, turn the little building next door into a laboratory, and do some research. And a year later, I'd invented a very unusual

nutrient for animals—Grain Number One, as I decided to call it. Of course Grain Number One was not exactly a grain. Or you could say it was a very tasty sort of grain that was saturated with a chemical compound I'd created. And then I hired some other young doctors and scientists to help me, and we hired a few more, and then, crossing all the boundaries of nationalities and continents, we hired a few more, and ultimately in not too many years we'd figured out how to use Grain Number One, in all its different forms, to create food where there'd been no food—starting by quietly giving a certain group of frogs an injection of it, after which their bodies could easily process a porridge we fed them that was made up entirely out of other frogs—and then moving on to forcing a certain variant of it into the upper atmosphere, so that an odd sort of rain began sprinkling down onto fields full of cows, with the result that cows who formerly had lived only off grass within several months were living happily off skunks and rats and foxes instead—and et cetera et cetera et cetera et cetera—that turned out to be the work of our generation. Grain Number One enabled ninety percent of the existing animal species on earth, including eighty percent of the herbivores, to achieve astonishing efficiency in chemically breaking down the flesh of other animals, including the flesh of members of their own species, dramatically reducing their need to consume plants. And once the capacity of the animals for processing various foods had changed, simple Pavlovian conditioning then led them to change their former eating habits as well, and we soon saw the pressure on the planet's dwindling supply of plants and pasture land being drastically alleviated, while animals that could be used as basic nourishment for humans were suddenly multiplying in astounding numbers. Grain Number One seemed to be the key to unlocking some sort of molecular inhibition, so that the animals who consumed it grew stronger and sleeker than they'd ever been before. There was an initial period of months or years after an animal's first contact with Grain Number One when you could observe in their behavior an almost mind-boggling vitality. Pigs, for example, would frequently have sexual intercourse fifteen or sixteen times every single day. And sometimes they'd engage in different sorts of sexual experimentation that had never been previously observed in pigs. Now, in some animals, this strange liveliness sometimes diminished, or was even replaced by a sort of lethargy or torpor, and sometimes the ability of the animals to recognize familiar things was slightly impaired, but the ease with which these animals could process animal matter never declined. And so it had to be said—we had changed the world. And of course, those of us in the original company, and certainly the company's founder, myself, derived some benefit from what we'd done, and—well—we became, as you might imagine, quite wealthy. And of course in a moderate way I tried some of the forms of my compound myself in the early days, I have to admit—don't tell me you wouldn't have. It was an amazing time. So before I'd even celebrated my thirty-ninth birthday, Grain Number One had spread through the water and the soil, and then it was everywhere. Anyway, here is the very first picture in the book.

(He takes out a mechanical device and touches a button on it. On a screen behind him, an image appears. The image is a picture of him when he was in his thirties, accompanied by an amusing-looking dog.)

This was one of our earliest successes, because my good friend Rufus here was the very first large mammal ever to be raised entirely on the meat of members of his own species. God, I must say—ha ha ha—showing you this illustrative image on a screen reminds me immediately of my long-ago school days and of my favorite old alcoholic biology teacher, Mr. Matthews. Ha ha ha. And I always remember how old Mr. Matthews used to say to us with such a strange expression on his face, "Boys and girls, man has two basic needs—the need for food and the need for sex." Ha ha ha— *(He's suddenly overwhelmed by a wave of dizziness)* Do you know, I still feel awfully dizzy . . .

(He goes to sit on the sofa, bringing his mechanical device and a small box along with him. He sits silently for a moment, then takes an odd disk out of the box and holds it up for the audience to see.)

I brought this with me. It's a letter from my wife to Rose. I found it lying around in the house, and I took it, and now I'm going to look at it. I know it's wrong to read someone else's mail, but you see, I spent half my life looking for clues about Cerise, because I didn't understand her. She eluded me, she escaped me. I don't mean only that from our earliest days together she'd leave the house at odd hours or unex-pectedly go off to some distant part of the globe. It was more than that. I mean, there were times when she and I would sit down to have a cup of coffee, and for moments, for whole minutes, it would be as if the two of us had become one glowing soul, flying through the universe together, but then suddenly I'd feel her flying off in some different direction towards some unknown destination, and I'd be sitting there next to her, wondering where she'd gone. Or maybe I was the one who was flying off—I could never be totally sure. But I kept having the comical thought that maybe Cerise was one of those people who led a secret life or something. And then she moved out into the middle of the woods. Well, she sent Rose this letter about a year ago.

(He inserts a disk into the device, and a film of Cerise appears on the screen. Cerise looks unwell. She is seated somewhere outside in a bleak landscape. She speaks to the camera.)

CERISE

(On film) "Dearest Rose, I'll only write a very few words. I told you too much yesterday about the sick wolf and the sick dogs and the horrible sounds they made as they cried out in pain. But I saw such a sight this afternoon as I was walking on the path between the elm tree and the brook. In fact I tripped and almost fell right into it—a pile of dead squirrels, at least a hundred of them, huddled together, with a few still alive but too sick to move. It's everywhere— everywhere. I miss you very much. Please write to me."

(The film fades out.)

HE

That's a strange letter, isn't it. What's she talking about? *(He gets up slowly and heads back to the lectern and picks up the bottle)* God, I think I need a bit more of this. *(He pours some and drinks. His mood grows suddenly jollier)* There we go! Ha ha ha. —So at any rate, I was describing the invitation that I'd received, and my sneezing fit, and— well—after that, I left my breakfast table, and I went into my bedroom, and I guess what I actually did then, frankly, was that I turned on all the lights, and I took off my bathrobe, and I looked at my dick. Well, that was enlivening. And then, I mean, to go through this precisely, I guess the next thing I did was that I sat down in my favorite armchair, and I was naked, of course, and somehow that made me start thinking about the whole history of women taking their clothes off in public, which is a subject that's always fascinated me. Well, because, you see, in the city where I grew up—and where I got older—there were really, up until twenty years ago or so, only two theaters where women did that: there was The Dome Of Life, over in what was called the flower district, and then there was a beautiful place called Fruit Salad With Cream that was actually only three blocks away from my own house, which was on a wonderful street called Pushbroom Lane. And you see, there were so many changes in the styles and practices of that incredible art form in the course of my life, and many of the changes started in that very theater. Because you see, I can remember back to the time when the girls at that theater would strip, and the men would just sit in the audience fully clothed. Ha ha ha. —And then I can remember the time, many years later, after I was forty or so, when the strippers began begging the men in the audience to pull down their trousers and show their penises, and then I can remember the time not long after that when the girls began to coax the men and cajole them into masturbating openly during the shows. Ha ha ha! Yes, you see, because masturbation itself was much less common then. Oh yes—I mean, you know, when I was a boy, for example, well, parents never masturbated in front of their children. In fact, children never masturbated in front of their parents!

And children of course would *never* make out with their parents or fuck them, ever, because that would have been seen as utterly shocking. Ha ha ha ha! —You see, when I was around forty, there was a relatively brief period of change in social customs, and quite a few things actually changed permanently then, but I'd have to say that up *until* that point, you see, and during the whole period of time when I was growing up, well, people simply didn't think very much about their genitals at all—I'm telling you the truth. And they didn't talk about them. So for me, you see, the way things eventually developed seemed quite extraordinary—the way people began to talk about their penises and vaginas in such detail at dinner parties and in magazines and in interviews—not just actors, but statesmen and political leaders—"my penis," "my vagina"—well, it was all suddenly so different. And I mean, somehow at that time, I actually became much more interested in my *own* genitals. And even as the years passed and I began to lose interest in quite a few things, I never quite lost interest in my own dick. Ha ha ha! And certainly if you'd asked me, I always would have said, "Well, yes, of course, my dick is my friend, and, actually, my dick is my *best* friend, and in a certain way, it's my *only* friend."

Ha ha ha. —And of course the funny thing was that I always knew that my friend—my best friend and perhaps my only friend—was actually quite funny-looking. I knew that. Of course. Because a penis simply never can be or will be as elegant or as beautiful as a foot, say, or a hand, or a face, or—not to mention—a woman's breast. A penis by its nature is simply funny. Odd, you know. Odd and funny. I never got used to the way it looked. I was always surprised. And yet, all the same, I did think my friend had a wonderful face. It was so simple—no eyes, no nose, just a simple mouth, permanently fixed in a sort of sad, wistful smile . . .

And, well, of course, my relationship with my dick was not just a friendship, as you can imagine. It was actually a love affair—an affair so intense that there was hardly room for anyone else. And of course I always believed that to be involved with another human being was a marvelous thing—but there was always that moment of, "Yes, I love you, but now please go away, because I need to spend time alone with my friend."

And I know what you're thinking, so I have to say that I was never tempted to live homosexually. I mean, I always knew that two dicks in one house would be one too many, because I would never have loved any other dick the way I loved my own. I would have seen it much too objectively. And I wouldn't have known what to do with the person on the other end of it, you see. In other words, I always knew that the very best thing about *my* dick was that the person on the other end of it was only me. I could be alone with my own dick, in other words, which I certainly couldn't have been with anyone else's.

And of course I loved to be alone. I loved it, loved it—I loved it more than anything in the world. I loved to be alone, but best of all, I loved to be alone *with a friend*, but that was really only possible with one *particular* friend, and that was my oldest, closest friend.

God, I remember how we'd go on these incredible vacations, just the two of us. Oh, there was a beautiful one when we went to France—we had a wonderful time. And I remember, one day in the shower, my friend got all excited, as sometimes happened, and I suddenly thought to myself, My God, you're scary. Because my friend looked violent, extreme, almost out of control. But then I thought, Well, really, it's a fantastic thing that a respectable, well-mannered person like me can have such a massive, powerful, and fearless friend. Ha ha ha!

So anyway, you see, I'd always loved nudity, including nude performances, because what other pleasures can we get in life except from what is naked, or, in other words, from getting closer and closer to what we call Nature? And when Cerise and I were first married she'd come along to some of those performances. We'd have a few drinks, and she'd enjoy herself. But at some point, that stopped.

(He sits on the sofa silently for a moment. He seems to grow weak and dizzy again. Cerise appears.)

CERISE

Well. Hello.

HE

My God, you look beautiful. How are you, darling?

CERISE

Not too bad.

HE

I've missed you so much. Why haven't you come to see me? What are you up to these days?

CERISE

I told you all that yesterday!

HE

What? You did? Did I see you yesterday?

CERISE

You don't remember seeing me yesterday?

HE

Well, I really don't remember yesterday at all.

CERISE

So you don't remember going to a party in the afternoon?

HE

No, no.

CERISE

Well, I told you, I've been very busy. I've been traveling. All over.

HE

Really.

CERISE

Yes, don't you remember, I showed you all the photographs I'd taken on my travels.

HE

Really.

CERISE

Yes, don't you remember, I gave you my photograph album, and then you forgot all about it and left it behind. I've brought it back for you.

HE

Oh good, good.

(She gives him an album in a little black cloth bag. He tucks it into a corner of the sofa and thinks for a moment. Cerise speaks to the audience.)

CERISE

He was quite a bit older than me, you see. I met him when he was around forty, and he'd just begun producing Grain Number One in vast quantities, and his company was growing, and he was making money, and he was becoming—I'm serious—terribly amusing. No, really, people were attracted to him. They found him magnetic, delightful. I did, too. And it was such an extraordinary period. Everyone was in such a state of excitement. Everyone was always saying, "I feel so full of life!" It was the time when people wore those sort of shimmering fabrics—silver, gold, red and purple—and there were parties where people would stay up all night long, and he always was at the center of them. People would cluster all around him as he talked about his work. And then someone would start to play some music, and everyone would dance, and some people would go off into different quiet little rooms together for a while, and then everyone would slowly regroup and gather around him again, and he would talk some more. But then that period ended, and people grew more tense, and he did, and I did. Actually, I kept a diary around that time, and I wrote quite a bit about sexual things, about some of the difficult experiences we had. *(She takes out her diary and reads from it)* "'Please stop! Stop!' I shouted loudly as I pulled away. Why was I suddenly so incredibly upset? For a moment I held his face, I looked into his eyes. Then we both fell back, and I lay in one corner of the bed, and he lay in the corner diagonally across from me, and he stared at me horribly and caressed himself with a dreadful expression on his face." *(She looks through the diary and finds another section)* Oh yes, this was from a time when we were staying at an inn way out in the country somewhere: "It's nice here, a simple bare room—a big bed, two tiny tables on either side of it. I was drinking water from a metal cup. We were sitting on top of the bed, naked—a hot night outside, with thunder rumbling. As he talked, I thought, Why should I listen, because I don't know him. But then I heard it—the hostility, the hate. It was as if I'd been shot, as if I'd been hit in the belly, and there was blood everywhere. Meanwhile, our genitals rested very simply on the bed as if they were ordinary parts of our bodies, like elbows or feet." *(She speaks to the audience)* But you see, it wasn't entirely in my nature, in any case, to live in a city, to live with a man. I'd get dragged down into all of it, I'd start feeling—I don't know—nervous, domesticated, trapped indoors in all those rooms, and I'd begin to feel the need to change shape for a while. And so I started taking trips to hot, sunny places. I'd go to some very clean, very quiet hotel, and in the afternoons I'd lie under the slowly creaking ceiling fan, sometimes quite happy, sometimes crying, and I'd feel my bones and muscles twisting and stretching, and then I'd fall into an incredibly deep sleep. *(Now she takes out another book and continues to speak to the audience)* By the way, can I ask, do you know this book, *Facts about Cats* by L. B. Buttons? God, I'm such a fan. *(She reads from it)* "Cats have wonderful lives. They really like to do the things they do. They like to chase mice, of course. And they like to tease mice—they *really* like to tease them. And everyone knows that they particularly like to punish mice, whether they're inflicting capital punishment or life imprisonment without the possibility of parole, or whatever type of punishment they're inflicting. It's a great life. In other words: cats tease mice, they play with them, and they punish them. They pummel them, and they eat them. But what's not generally known is that cats also sometimes protect mice. They protect them, they comfort them, they pardon them, and sometimes they reward them, way beyond what any person would think they deserve."

Well, that's the thing about Nature, isn't it? It provides grace, beauty, and joy quite unexpectedly, and it even returns good for evil. All the time.

Now, Buttons writes quite a lot about the fact that cats can change their form and how all of that works. But there's one thing he leaves out of his book, for whatever reason. He doesn't mention the very important fact that cats mate for life. That's right. You heard me. They mate for life. Like humans.

You see, the bonds that cats form don't ever break, though they may change shape. And even though cats have more than one life, well, every time they cross over that barrier of death, they carry those particular connections right along with them.

(She leaves. He remains sitting on the sofa for a while, not feeling well. Finally he goes to the lectern, pours a bit more of the liquid, and drinks.)

HE

Excellent! *(He feels better and speaks to the audience)* No one who hasn't made money can possibly imagine how exciting it is. If you haven't experienced it, you just can't know how much pleasure you can get from receiving enormous checks. I mean, at that incredible moment when the checks really started pouring in, I just felt that everything, *everything*, was there to be taken. Whatever I wanted, I could have. It was all for me.

(Robin appears.)

ROBIN

Hello, sweetheart.

HE

Wonderful, wonderful. *(To the audience)* I met Robin when I was in my early forties, and the company's expansion had become exponential.

(She sits beside him on the sofa. She looks around at the audience and then speaks.)

ROBIN

(To the audience) Well, I'm sure that many of you married people here tonight have certainly had a love affair or two in the course of your marriage. Isn't that right? I mean, after all, when you think about the trends in the world today, a love affair is hardly— *(She looks around the audience)* Whoops!—maybe you're not quite ready to talk about that now. I'm sorry. I take it all back. What I meant to say was, I'm sure that you certainly *haven't* done anything like that, so you won't know what I'm talking about when I refer to the special coziness of waking up in a bed which is really not yours, and feeling the touch on your skin of sheets that aren't yours, and then going with your lover to a neighborhood café which in a sense very particularly *is* yours, even

though, really, it's not your neighborhood . . . Well, people always tell these romantic stories about how they met. —You know, "I was wandering alone through a glade of fir trees deep in the Garden of the Sacred Shrubs, and I heard someone singing to themselves quietly in a sad little voice, and I wondered, Who could be singing so quietly and sadly, and"—ha ha ha ha! Well, our story wasn't like that at all! Ha ha ha. —We met at a party, like so many people. And at the time I met him, I happen to have been terribly worried about this rash I'd developed, and, well, the dermatology office I ordinarily went to was booked for a month, and so at this party, somebody told me, "Well, that guy over there is actually a doctor." So I said, "Please introduce me." And when I met him I simply begged him to see me, even though he told me he wasn't really practicing anymore and just did research. "Do some on me," I said, even though he was hardly my type, and I think his mind must have started running in some odd direction, because when I went to his office the next day, late in the afternoon, he examined me in a very awkward and sort of clumsy manner. There was something unprofessional about the way he moved this rather homemade-looking instrument all around my upper body, while constantly bumping into my thigh with what seemed to be this enormous erection. As he looked at my rash, he was sort of talking compulsively about his wife and his marriage, laughing nervously again and again at his own remarks. At any rate, I was quite relieved when he finally prescribed some lotions and creams, and the appointment was over. And then we went out together into the gray light of dusk.

Part Two

He and Robin are seated on the sofa.

HE

(To the audience) On the night I examined Robin in regard
to that rather minor dermatological problem, Cerise was far
away, lying on some beach in Greece, and Robin's husband
Mike happened to have been held over in Japan—some
problem in his company, they were based there, you know.
And so without much discussion, Robin and I walked out
of my office together, and then we walked down the street
together, and then somehow we found ourselves walking
into a very quiet restaurant that we happened to pass, and
we had some dinner there and drank some wine. And after
dinner, both of us drunk, we resumed our walk, and we
came to a neighborhood neither of us knew. We wandered
through tangles of narrow streets and explored and talked.
And as we seemed to be caught in a sort of cul-de-sac by
a large park, she suddenly said something which I found

quite insulting—she said, "I think you're a shit, because I think you just want to use me to get away from your wife," or words to that effect—and we stood still in the street and stared at each other. There was no one else around, no one awake in the city but us, it seemed.

Her face had the clarity of water at dusk. Splash! I struck it lightly. Splash! Splash!

I grabbed her shirt by the neck with both hands, and there were tiny little clicks as a button delicately fell to the street and rolled and hit the side of a building and stopped.

I opened my mouth and went for her neck; I could see my face as a dog's face. Then her face became a dog's face, too. Her jaws opened, teeth bared. We went into the park, I pulled down my trousers, and I was sucked inside her with a slurping noise almost before we hit the ground. My hands pulled grass as we banged back and forth in the wet mud. Then we got up slowly, genitals dripping, and covered ourselves. Right outside the park, there was a small hotel; we went in, went up to a room, and, without stopping to turn on the light, we found the bed, pulled our clothes down, and fucked once again.

Then she fell into a deep sleep, but I lay beside her twisting around. When I got up and put on the clothes I'd just been wearing, my underpants felt like a disordered room where a party had been held, the champagne and confetti not yet cleared away. I washed my face. It was two A.M. Suddenly, she woke up and looked at me. I said in a whisper, *(To Robin)* "I'm sorry I disturbed you. Just go back to sleep. I'm stepping out for a minute."

ROBIN

(To the audience) He slipped out of the room like a fish swimming silently through aisles of coral. How long did

34

I lie there? Water was dripping from a washcloth in the bathroom. I fell back to sleep.

HE

(To the audience) Without knowing why, I went back into the park, and I started to run. Rain was pouring down. I was in a forest, horses were wandering through a lake. I pulled myself up onto one of them, and we rode off through the trees in the freezing rain at an incredible speed. My clothes were soaked, even my shoes. Branches roughly scratched my face as we rode on and on, faster and faster, apparently traveling into the deepest wilderness, where the trees were almost terrifyingly large. Suddenly I saw a light, glowing in the distance. It was a huge castle. I rode up to it, got off my horse, found a door, and went inside. I was reeling, dizzy, everything was dark and cold. Then there was a room—no light at all, but chairs were placed at an enormous table, and one of them was empty, so I sat down in it. Then I started to be able to see a bit—and I saw that sitting next to me there was a white cat with a striped face and small, twirling eyes, and she was so beautiful that, when I looked at her, for a moment I felt I was going to pass out. Then I could see that seated at the table there were dozens of cats, all naked except for the ribbons around their necks. Clearly the white cat beside me, though, was different from the others, because unlike the green ribbons which the others wore, her ribbon was red. The room was filled with a hollow jingling sound—because the ribbons of the cats were decorated with bells—and the smell of the room was sharp and salty. Then a uniformed waiter brought me a large white plate holding three mice, served whole, in a creamy sauce. The mice lay nestling in a circle of rice, and the rice in

turn was rimmed by a crust of small vegetables. My stomach immediately began to turn over, and in a panic I cried out to the white cat beside me. "Please," I said, "you see, I'm terribly sorry to be impolite, but I can't eat mice. You see, in the place I come from, we don't eat mice. We—" A guard grabbed my shoulders, and another servant pressed my right forearm flat against the table, palm down. Then the white cat beside me slowly picked up a scalpel-like knife and drew a line with it across the back of my hand. There was a short silence, and then agonizing pain started to pour out of the wound. For a moment the white cat stared at the neat little slit with its rapidly flowing blood. Then she dragged the back of her paw across the wound, and it was sealed off. Then she licked the blood off her paw. And after that, I wasted no time in starting to eat.

The meat was delicious—tart, savory, and they cooked their mice rare. Imitating the others at the table, I saved the head for last and ate it in one bite. And imitating the others again, I dropped the tails into one of several small buckets set out on the table.

At a certain point in the meal, I felt the white cat's paw move onto my leg. Playing with my testicles humorously and slowly, she watched me eating the mice, a drunken, drowsy expression wavering on her face. Then somehow her paw had extracted my member from inside my trousers, and my astonished penis was completely enclosed in a warm coat of indescribable coziness, such as travelers dream of on snowy nights. When I turned towards her, all of a sudden she stared into my eyes, penetrating me so deeply and fully that I felt turned inside out, and she just kept on looking at me. My God—finally. Finally, to be known, I thought, as hot sperm flowed out of me, flowing over her paw as if it would never stop. To be seen and known. I was weeping with gratitude, but of course it was funny, too, as I tried to use my dinner napkin with my left hand for my eyes and nose as *well* as for my penis, which was now dripping onto the stone floor below me, while at the same time I pretended with my right hand still to be eating my meal. Finally she gave my arm a little tug, and I followed her out through a swinging door, then up some flights of stairs and down some hallways to a tiny dark bedroom, where, sitting beside her on a rather gorgeous bedspread on a large bed, I buried my face in her neck, my tears flowing freely once again, her bony little shoulder just touching my cheek. As I moved above her, I was sweating and trembling, my member slowly finding its way through her unfamiliar fur and attempting penetration. For quite a while I was pressing gently against something hard, twisting and turning to no avail, and I was horribly afraid, in my state of excitement, that I'd come too soon; then something suddenly unlocked inside her, my penis went in with ease, and we made love, until an intense orgasm came up from my toes, and I completely blacked out.

I awoke quite quickly, or I felt I did, and I found my hands exploring the fur of her face. Her whiskers, mouth, tongue. "My love, my love," I murmured again and again. And then I lay back against some pillows, and she found herself a comfortable spot where she could sit on top of me, her little asshole almost touching my navel. I noticed a large bottle of champagne on the night table next to the bed, with an empty bowl beside it. I opened the bottle with a loud pop and poured some champagne into the bowl. She walked across me, lowered her head, and drank, and then I drank, too. And while I drank, she was licking my chest, then my palm, my fingers, and my hand stained the sheets with cat and champagne.

When I came back outside, the horse was waiting, and the trip back through the forest seemed to take only moments. Leaving the horse in the park, I soon was creeping back into the silent hotel room, where Robin was sleeping. Dawn was just beginning to break. Robin rolled over in bed. I got in beside her and hugged her and kissed her. "My darling," I said. "My darling. My darling."

ROBIN

(To the audience) I slowly woke up to the sound of his voice. I turned on the lights and dressed in front of him.

HE

I was astounded, obviously, by the amount of hair which surrounded her cunt. My heart pounded and swelled.

During the following week, my mood was unsettled. I was irritable, jumpy. Cerise had finally returned from Greece, but things continued to be difficult between us. My colleagues noticed that I was always on the phone. Robin insisted on going away secretly for a weekend with me, and I agreed. She told elaborate lies to her husband, Mike, and I to Cerise. And on a Friday afternoon, I left work early, got on a train, and got off at the station Robin had named, and when I stepped on to the platform, she was waiting for me, disguised in the practical gray raincoat of a suburban wife. She drove me through a landscape of hills and meadows until we turned off onto a dirt road and rumbled to the side of a large lake where a little rowboat was quietly bobbing in the water. And then we got in the boat, she handed me the oars, and we rowed across to a small island. On the island there was just one house, not large but quite modern in style. We walked in the door and put down our things. Everywhere you looked, there were bright clean surfaces, with sharply sprouting plants—just like her clean, shiny body with its pubic hair. And then she took my hand and led me up a flight of steps to a small room under a sloping roof, where a bed with sparkling white sheets was waiting for us. She sat down on the bed, I sat in a chair, she removed her shoes, and I removed mine. Then she leaned rather languorously back against the headboard of the bed and watched without moving as I awkwardly started to take off my clothes. It seemed awfully funny. Eventually she burst into roars of laughter. Then, rather pensively, she too undressed. I got on the bed, and as we started to embrace, I noticed on the floor, so far below us, all of our clothes, in their arbitrary pattern, as they'd fallen—what awfulness, what falseness they represented: everything in the world which we supposedly were but really were not—how easily a sociologist could look at that pile of shirts, trousers, and underwear and calculate our exact location in the long parade of the human race—how easily he could guess the period we'd lived in, the name of our city, and even our beliefs, the music we listened to, the books we liked—but it wasn't really right! Of course, when we were twenty, when we were twenty-two, we'd reached into the heap of available thoughts and available attitudes and grabbed different things to cover our nakedness, but we always knew they weren't really what we wanted. We'd always planned to return one day and revise it all, but we never had. Naked on the bed, we forgot all the things we'd decided we were and said we were—we started again. I wasn't the person I'd always pretended to be—I was hardly a particular person at all.

It was hot in the little room when we finally woke up, and brilliant with sunlight. Saturday was so short that we never got dressed. We held on to each other, we ate, we silently stared at each other. We even went outside and looked around a little, without putting on our clothes. Late in the afternoon, we were wading through the mud at the edge of the island, and we heard a loud rustling and froze, terrified. It sounded like there was a huge creature approaching through the trees—something enormous— maybe a bear—but when it finally appeared, it was a hilarious badger, waddling in our direction! "Give it some food," you laughed out hysterically. I pulled a banana out of the bag I was carrying, quickly peeled it, and tossed it towards the badger. He ran away from it, as fast as he could. We screamed like hyenas, it seemed so funny.

That night, it was cold—brutally cold, with an icy wind. It was as if we felt wet as we lay in our bed. We hugged each other tightly but kept on shivering. So she went to a drawer and pulled out two pairs of funny pajamas with a design of rabbits. They were marvelously warm!—but they were the beginning of the end. The next day, Sunday, it was gray and rainy, and so we put on some clothes—our own, naturally—and by late afternoon we were talking once again about the lives we called "ours." The things we'd chosen. Thoughts. Selves. The city. The beliefs. The music. The books. The husband. The wife.

ROBIN

We began an affair. We rented a rather expensive, rather sensual, slightly vulgar furnished apartment way out by Glove Park.

HE

Cerise bought a cabin way out in the middle of the woods somewhere, in some remote mountainous area, full of brooks and streams. She went there more and more often, and when I finally told her I wanted to live with Robin, Cerise decided to move to her cabin for good.

ROBIN

So I brought everything over to Pushbroom Lane, including the paintings, the plants, and all the wonderful bright lamps I'd collected for years. I filled the place with soft sofas, soft pillows. And in the newly reborn house, I tried to make something like a home for him. A shrine, almost, to the cult of the penis. I gave him a bath each night before dinner, set out the bathroom with candles and oils, washed the penis gently and lovingly in the warm bath, then dressed him in a thick white robe and brought him his food on a table in the bedroom—a cutlet, maybe, or noodles, his favorite. Then we'd walk very quietly over to the bed, I'd present myself to him, splaying out on the satin sheets, and we'd kiss each other, make out, and fuck.

HE

A year passed, and I was well, I was happy. But then one night a sharp pain in my arm woke me suddenly, and I rushed into the bathroom and saw bleeding lines on my skin. I'd been roughly scratched. Without even thinking, I dressed quickly and silently, taking the greatest care not to wake Robin, and then I slipped out the door and ran as fast as I could towards the green park.

So, life with Robin went on as before. But now every few weeks, after we'd gone to bed, I'd get up and sneak out of the house, and pretty soon I'd find myself riding on a horse through the deep wilderness with the enormous trees all the way out to that cold stone castle, so dark and so silent in the middle of the night that it seemed deserted, and I'd make my way through the completely lightless hallways to my white cat's room, I'd climb into her bed and grab hold of her thick white tail with both of my hands, and I'd wake her up, and we'd embrace for hours and murmur to each other in our secret way. Occasionally she'd take me out to a late-night show in some odd sub-basement below the palace—or every once in a while we'd climb into her enormous sleigh-like vehicle and fly off to some marvelously painted theater where the walls and even the sets were made of jewels, or else to some rough, shack-like structure way out in the darkness of the forest somewhere. Because apparently there were performances there of every description—plays and operas and satirical cabarets—all available all night long for any lost souls who might happen to be awake. Once she took me to a puppet show that was filled with choral singing. As five hundred or so voices started to slither around each other in a weird, high, silvery harmony, tears instantly began falling down my face.

From the way the other cats behaved towards her, I sometimes wondered if my white cat was somehow running the whole place, and I thought, if she was, she was awfully clever about it, because it all seemed to be so prosperous and peaceful.

Robin didn't seem to notice my late-night excursions. She seemed quite content.

And so, many years passed in the same way.

ROBIN

Again and again, I'd wake up suddenly in the middle of the night, and he wouldn't be there. I'd lie in bed, confused and upset, and then, hours later, I'd see him returning from wherever he'd been, moving around stealthily so as not to wake me. Usually he'd go into the bathroom to undress, but occasionally he'd stand near the window instead, and more than once I noticed, when he took his clothes off, that his member seemed to be an odd color and looked strangely bruised. One night I broke out of our usual routine. I told him I felt sick and had to go to bed early. After we ate, I kissed him gingerly, holding him carefully at arm's length. Then I slipped under the covers and closed my eyes. This was all a ruse. Underneath my pajamas I wore an elaborate disguise—male clothing, with a large rubber dick inside my black trousers. Of course he pretended to go to sleep, too. Then a couple of hours later, he slipped out of bed and began to dress. When he finally left the room, I shed my pajamas, slipped on some shiny black formal men's shoes which I'd carefully hidden, and followed quickly behind him. I followed him out into the park till we reached a meadow where bright white moonlight fell on pastel-colored ponies, pink and yellow. Some of them were seated, some playing cards, others were running; and it started to rain. He mounted one of the ponies, I jumped on another. In the freezing rain I followed him through a rocky land-scape, splashing through rivers at terrifying speed, until we reached a large palace, and he hurried inside. When I followed him in, I found myself in a gaily decorated room where a sort of children's party was taking place. I had no time to wonder where he'd gone, because I was immediately surrounded by a group of brightly costumed young animals, who seemed to be greeting me and welcoming me to the party. Then a thin dog in a sailor hat bounded towards me with a vile grin on his ugly face. He handed me a plate of hotcakes and proceeded to look at me with a brazen, open-mouthed carnality, staring into my eyes while pouring syrup onto my plate from an enormous pitcher. Just as the syrup was about to spill on to the floor, I handed the plate back to the drooling dog and rushed out of the room. A dark passageway led to a huge dining hall where adults were gathered—mostly men—and food was being served at a big long table. No one paid any attention to me, so I took a seat and helped myself to some of the beef stew which sat in large bowls all along the table. The dinner was not a very refined affair, because donkeys—asses—stood at the table, interspersed among the seated people, and while we tried to eat, they haphazardly pissed, making the floor an unholy mess—although I could tell that all the men found the dicks of the donkeys rather big and exciting, judging at least from the comments they made. After a while, I grew restless. I was sitting by chance next to a chef from the kitchen who had somehow gathered around him a coterie of cats. The cats wanted to know how every fucking dish was made. "Er—how is that prepared? Meow— Meow—" "Er—how is that prepared? —Meow— Meow—" For some reason, that irritated me.

HE

That night, my white cat behaved rather strangely. As I lay naked on the bed, my pulsating member pointing towards the ceiling, almost begging for sex, she prowled restlessly back and forth beside me, then suddenly crawled between the sheets and fell asleep. When I went downstairs, I found myself at a children's party, and for no good reason I found myself drying the tears of a sad little fawn—rather attractive, though—a sad little fawn who kept getting herself worked up over nothing. As soon as I would calm her down about one of her anxieties, something else would occur to her, and she'd start getting hysterical all over again. Finally, the clown came in with his enormous red artificial hands and throbbing red artificial nose. *That* she liked, and when she heard some of his jokes, she stopped sobbing and began to laugh. I must admit, he *was* funny, and between his jokes he turned me around and drilled my butt with his entirely unartificial big red dick, and I was yelling and making a hell of a noise. There were several maids there who brought around sandwiches, some of plain lettuce but some with tongue, and while everyone ate, several of the children played very naughty games, and one of the maids put her tray aside, held my cock, and gently jerked it around until I cheerfully came, while the clown and the little fawn watched us and laughed. Then I got frisky and fucked one of the maids in the ass, while all the other maids made a circle around us, cheering us on, and screaming and clapping as we had our orgasms. A bit later, I joined some of the cats in a small private room where a rather long table was fitted out for a late snack. On each plate there was an American-style doughnut, like a little pink automobile tire, and in the center of the doughnut, facing up, there was a mouse's head. As a joke, the cooks gave two or three of us men's penis heads instead. The cats found that fantastically funny, as they were mostly quite drunk. Eventually, they all leaned back in their comfortable chairs, their bellies showing, and closed their eyes. As they dozed off dreamily, I felt so relaxed that I pulled my pants down and simply laid my dick out flat on the table, where I found it extended surprisingly far. A few random thoughts or fantasies occurred to me, which lifted the dick right off the table, causing a shadow to form which fell across the faces of the cats and slightly confused them as they slept and dreamed. I watched them ineffectually trying to bat the shadow away as I slowly drifted off to sleep myself.

After an hour or so, I woke up, and I didn't feel very well. Placing my penis inside my trousers, I stumbled outside and mounted the pony which had brought me to the castle. My body ached all over.

ROBIN

Hours passed at the banquet table, and finally for dessert a large cake was served. It was nicely shaped, blond, with many layers, and it was thickly covered with a sticky green icing which was thoroughly enjoyed by both asses and men. By the end of the evening, many of the men were pissing and braying right along with the asses, and so no one noticed when I left the table, slipping out of the room through some furry dark curtains.

Instinct led me. I knew where I was going. There were no hesitations. Up flights of steps, down freezing cold hallways, on and on until a pungent smell told me I'd found the right room. I opened a simple, unlocked door, and there she was. She lay alone in sumptuous thick sheets, silver and gray, her soft little face, with its wonderful stripes, lying peacefully against a thin pillow. A guttering candle by the bed shed a soft yellow light. I stood and marveled at her, breathing in her overwhelming perfume. It was harsh and yet intoxicating, and I could almost feel my smooth rubber penis starting to stir. Forcing myself with difficulty out of my trance-like state, I pulled the heavy knife from where it lay between my breasts, and with all my strength, trembling, I brought it down in a furious stroke and cut off the cat's head. Blood sprayed out over the entire bed; it poured out and didn't stop. Leaving the head where it lay on the pillow, I carried the body into her own bathroom, held her by her back legs over her own bathtub, and shook her out till she was entirely drained. I grabbed a bag from her closet and stuffed the body into it, tail first. Outside, it was drizzling lightly, and my pony rocked me gently as we headed into the forest. Still clutching the bag with the cat's body in my right hand, I opened my pants with my left hand and caressed the penis, pressing it hard against my own genitals for a long time, and then I pulled it off and tossed it away. We rode gradually faster, the cold wind pleasant against my face. Midway through the trip, I reached into the bag and felt the cat's neck. A new head was already starting to grow.

(Music. Strange images appear on the screen. After a while the music and images go away, and Robin speaks.)

By taking some short cuts, I got home, as I'd hoped, while he was still out. I put the lumpy sack in the back of our closet. Then I undressed, washed, and got in bed, naked. I caressed myself and masturbated, taking a pleasure in my own body which was rare for me, and the orgasms that slowly arose were both simple and deep, like well-earned rewards after hard work. After a while, he came in, and I feigned sleep. He was breathing noisily, almost wheezing, his face a mask of something like despair. He dropped into an armchair, tossing and turning, as if he were writhing in pain. In the morning, when I woke up, he was already

awake, lying beside me, an expression of mindless igno-
rance and idiocy on his face. I told him I had a surprise
to show him. I got out of bed and left the room. Then
I came back in, holding the trembling cat against my naked
breasts. "This is Blanche. I found her on the street and
took pity on her," I said, referencing an emotion I wasn't
known for.

Have you ever seen anyone actually "grow pale"?
Because that is exactly what happened to the poor dumb
fuck. Have you ever seen anyone's "flesh crawl"? I swear
I saw his do exactly that. The poor cat's head had grown
in without stripes, just what you might call the shadows
of stripes. I put her down on the floor, and she hobbled
towards him, a totally fucked-up version of a domestic
pussy. He smiled very weakly, then he left the room quickly
for the hall bathroom, from which the sounds of vomiting
soon emerged. "Do you know, my stomach hasn't been
right since we had dinner at Luigi's," was the first thing he
said when he came back into the bedroom, huge beads of
sweat making a perfect circle around his head, as if he were
a sickly king who had just removed his crown. And from
that moment on, unfortunately, I never knew him to have
a full week of perfect health. Something strange was wrong
with him. And strangely, I happened to know exactly what
it was. I'd always loved eccentric, self-published books
by people on the fringes of science, people who taught at
obscure experimental colleges and whose articles didn't
appear in the mainstream journals, but who nonetheless
sometimes posed extremely daring and penetrating ques-
tions. So I happened to be one of the few people around to
notice—much less read—Harley Granville's book, *Nature
Fights Back*. I was intrigued by its one-line description in

the catalog, "Possible Consequences of Grain Number One," and so I ordered a copy. In a quiet manner, Granville simply pointed out that since Grain Number One gave the digestive system of an awful lot of animals some remarkably powerful, almost explosive, chemical tools to play around with, a question did arise about whether those rather unattractive and charmless beings that we call microorganisms, you know, bacteria and viruses, might not just possibly be a bit more sensitive and a bit more easily offended than they're given credit for, and, if so, whether perhaps in response to the disruption of their lives inflicted on them by Grain Number One, they might just possibly adapt in certain ways that would be harmful to other forms of life. Granville spoke frankly of the sickness and death of the human species, and then, in an epilogue, he predicted the sickness and death of other species as well. In his opinion, it would all spread. I never mentioned that I'd read the book—but of course it was obvious that if there was going to be a sickness caused by Grain Number One, the first person to be affected by it might very well be him.

HE

My stomach remained distinctly disturbed. Days passed, then weeks, then three or four years, and I couldn't seem to recover entirely. "God knows what Luigi must have put in that spaghetti," I used to say all the time, with diminishing humor. Going to the office each day seemed more and more difficult, more and more irritating, and less and less interesting, so not too long after my fiftieth birthday, I sold my share of the company and said good-bye to all that. In any case, I was tired all the time, exhausted really. I wasn't so sick that I couldn't leave the house, but as there was now nothing terribly pressing that I had to do, I fell into the habit of spending my days for the most part in bed. Morning after morning, as Robin left for work, she would awaken me by kissing me on the lips. Sometimes her kisses were wet and tempting, and as her breasts fell over my face, I'd sort of reach out to touch them, and she'd always pull away. And then she'd leave, and there I'd be, alone all day in the house with Blanche—Blanche, this strange, sickly, uninteresting cat whom I didn't like. And as the years passed, the days in those overheated, airless rooms, where I never wore clothes, seemed to grow longer and longer. For hours at a time, Blanche would sit perched on top of my curled-up dick. Perhaps once or twice a day I'd get slightly aroused, she'd wriggle herself discreetly off of me on to the sheet, I'd laboriously jerk off, and she'd watch, casually. Every once in a while I'd intentionally hit her with the sperm, which was sometimes droll. Sure, I was drinking, but drinking could only soften the edges of things, and by late afternoon, I'd usually be weak with nausea, making my way often into the bathroom to vomit, then lying quite still on the bathroom floor till I vomited again. Just before Robin would come home each night, I'd brush my teeth and put on a shirt and trousers—at first it sort of amused me to see how long I could get away with wearing the same ones before Robin would ask, "Are you sure you've done the laundry?" Ha ha ha. —I felt at that time that Robin and Blanche were working together, and it made sense to imagine that Blanche possessed a very particular power—a power often referred to in casual conversation, but always as a joke. In real life, I knew, it wouldn't have been funny, not at all. Because I felt Blanche had the power, the capability, of literally being able to bore someone to death.

ROBIN

At night I'd come home, and he'd clearly feel ill and much too weak, he'd imply, to have sex with me. Sometimes he'd beg me to masturbate in front of him. I'd always decline. And then he'd beg me to watch his own masturbation. I usually said no, but sometimes I would, and it was pitiful how much he wanted me to find in watching the act, how much he himself wanted to find in doing it. On those pointless evenings, I would stare at his member. I'd watch him caress it. I'd look and look. But there were no answers in there. It didn't talk, it didn't say *anything*. No answers at all. He wanted it to speak, to really tell him what he needed to know, as if the sperm spilling out of it could be thought or feeling, an idea, happiness, some service to humanity, completion, love. But the sperm was only sperm, and there was nowhere else he could turn for help. I understood the problem. Everywhere he went, he was blocked by boredom. The boredom really was something unbeatable—who could fight that? No one could. He had no way out. What could break through it? I mean, what could he do? Could he kill someone? Well—maybe. Well, who? Me? Sure—I guess. Well, sure, he could. How would he do it? Stab me? Great. Why not? It would be amazing! The blood pouring out of me, hotter than coffee. My skin in shreds, the fullness of the screams. My voice without any inhibition at all. Would he have an orgasm? —You *bet* he would, the best of his life. The very best moment ever of his life. Pure joy. But *then* what? He'd be sitting there with my dead body—nothing he wanted. The whole fucking high would last fifteen minutes, and then he'd be back with his boredom and his dick.

HE

Occasionally, in order to avoid Blanche, I'd lock myself in the bathroom right after lunch. Sometimes I'd lie in the bathtub for hours, squirting water at my dick from different directions using a special nozzle attachment Robin had bought me, trying to delay my orgasms for as long as possible. Occasionally in the evenings, Robin would ask me if I wanted to go out somewhere—to some social gathering, a concert, or some sort of performance—but it always seemed too difficult. I was too worn out.

ROBIN

"What is boredom?" one might very well ask. I thought about that a lot at that time. I came to see it eventually as a sort of spiritual inability to digest the events that make up our lives so that they can be turned into the substance that gives us pleasure.

HE

One night I agreed to go to a dinner party just a few streets away, but almost as soon as we arrived at the party, Robin placed me very carefully at an enormous table full of people and then wandered off and disappeared into a swirling mob of guests. I had no idea how to behave, so I addressed myself totally to the plate in front of me, and, well, you know, the food wasn't bad—it was some sort of chicken—but I was having trouble breathing, and I must have been finding it difficult to hear properly, because the person next to me seemed to be trying to tell me his name, and it sounded as if he was saying that his name was Sentimental Melting Custard-Face Mouth-Droop. Robin never reappeared, and a long time passed with everyone talking and eating—maybe a few hours—and then I slowly began to realize that the discussion at the table was starting to repeat itself, word for word, and I myself was saying certain things for the second time. For some reason, that terrified me—I turned ice cold, I stood up in a crudely impolite manner, and I ran out of the party and out into the rain.

When I arrived at home, I found the cat walking nervously on top of the sofa, obviously at a loss or distracted somehow. Then I looked upstairs, and I saw Robin, also with the same distracted face, it seemed, coming out of the bedroom completely nude, her cunt dripping. Through the crack of the open bedroom door, I could see her husband Mike disconsolately covering his enormous member with a small bit of underwear. The hint of sexuality was unmistakable. "Perhaps I haven't come at an appropriate time," I began awkwardly, my own dick slightly lifted by the unexpected scene. Robin and her husband dismissed my remark with a sort of exhausted irritability, pulling on their clothes with abrupt movements.

The next night, I made dinner. *(He is cooking, chopping vegetables. To Robin)* So the guy—I'm sorry—what did you say? My attention somehow wandered for a moment. You were saying that Paul Hay—?

ROBIN

I said that Paul *Klee* was one of Jerry's favorite painters, so if you wanted to get a present for Ed, I saw a nice book of watercolors by Paul Klee, and if you—

HE

Why would I be getting a present for Fred?

ROBIN

For *Ed . . . Ed . . .*

HE

Oh. Ed. *(Silence. He chops vegetables)* Yes, I can remember a period when Jerry liked Klee. But that was a long time ago. I haven't heard Jerry say anything about Klee for at least ten years.

(As he prepares food, Robin prepares for her own suicide. She puts on music. A ritual is readied: a basin of water, soap, candles. As he moves on to the next stage of his cooking, she appropriates the knife and places it among the items she's assembling. After preparing a circle of objects on the floor, she stands in the center of it.)

What are you doing?

ROBIN

Nothing, obviously. *(She starts to undress)*

HE

Are you going somewhere?

ROBIN

No. *(She picks up the knife)*

HE

Well then, why are you— Fuck! —Will you stop that?

(She continues her action.)

Is this that suicide thing again?

ROBIN

Not—suicide—

(They stare at each other.)

HE

What's going on? What's happening? *What's happening?*

ROBIN

Ha ha ha ha— Ha ha ha ha— "What's happening? What's happening?" —Ha ha ha ha— That's becoming sort of like a slogan with you, isn't it, you seem to say it so frequently. Ha ha ha ha— It's like one of those phrases that fanatics use when they meet each other, like, "Heil Hitler!"— "What's happening? What's happening?" —Ha ha ha ha— Here's what's happening!

(She tries to stab him with the knife. They struggle, fight. He takes the knife from her. And it seems that he will kill her, but instead he throws the knife on the ground, then turns off the music.)

HE

Look, I'll tell you my problem. I'm terribly tired. I'm desperate to sleep, but I can't sleep. I—

ROBIN

You can't? Why not?

HE

I can't sleep, obviously, because Blanche wanders around all night long, she—

ROBIN

Really? She does?

HE

She knocks things over, she goes through every room—

ROBIN

Well, maybe we'd better get rid of her, then.

HE

What?—

ROBIN

I don't mean kill her, for Christ's sake. I just mean, maybe we should find another home for her—I don't know—write an ad or something . . .

HE

Really? Do you think so?

(He is gone. Rose is there instead. She and Robin are seated.)

ROBIN

(To Rose) Yes. I see.

(They are silent for a moment.)

Look—I—do you—do you mind my asking? ––Why do you want a cat, exactly?

(Rose looks funny.)

Do you like animals?

ROSE

Well—for my apartment, actually. You know—for mice. I just—I just—I hate mice.

ROBIN

Oh. Sure. Yes. I understand. But can I be frank with you? I love Blanche. I want to give her to someone who would also—love her.

ROSE

Well—mm—that's asking quite a lot . . . *(Giggles)* I'm not sure I can promise that. That might be a little too much for me . . . ha ha ha . . .

(They are silent for a moment.)

ROBIN

Look, I'll be honest with you. I don't care about the cat. That was sort of a pretext. I'm actually looking for a girl-friend for this man I know.

ROSE

Oh? You—

ROBIN

I've—I've sort of been living with him myself for a while, actually, but we're having some problems . . .

ROSE

Oh—I see.

ROBIN

(Handing her a large photograph) This is his penis.

ROSE

Wow. Nice.

ROBIN

(Taking back the picture) So—you're interested, then?

ROSE

"Interested" . . . well . . . I don't—I—

(He enters.)

HE

Hey!

ROBIN

(To Rose) Wait. What luck. This is him now.

HE

Oh—I'm sorry—am I—?—er—ah—

ROBIN

No, no—Rose has come to see about Blanche.

HE

Ah. I see. *(To Rose)* Are you going to take her?

ROSE

Well, the—

ROBIN

Possibly.

ROSE

(To Robin, getting up) So—er—just let me know how you feel about it. Give it some thought. Er—ah—here's my—er—here's my business card . . . It has a picture of—ah—my vagina on it. *(She gives a business card to each of them)*

ROBIN

Oh, great—thanks.

HE

Yes, great.

(Rose leaves.)

Well—I hope that girl will take Blanche. There's something agreeable about her, somehow.

ROBIN

Oh, you liked her, did you?

HE

Yes—I did.

ROBIN

Why is that, do you think?

HE

Oh, I don't know. She seemed quite nice—er—. . . and I—I—I guess I tend to be—you know—affectionate, and—er—

ROBIN

But you don't like Blanche, it seems. And you don't like me, we know that.

HE

What? How can you say that? I've ruined my life for you. Isn't that enough?

ROBIN

It's something, sure. It doesn't mean you like me.

HE

Mm . . . I see . . .

ROBIN

Anyway, be honest—*she's* the one who interests you now. Something's going to happen between you and her—I'd stake my life on it.

HE

Oh, come on.

ROBIN

Something—"sexual." God, I love that word. Ha ha ha—
(Robin leaves)

HE

The next morning, Robin gave Blanche to Rose. So during the nights I slept soundly, and by day I sat in my chair by the window, and once again spring came. In the mornings, amazingly, I'd sometimes wake up because very nice lips, covered with lipstick, were enclosing my member and play-ing with it briefly, and sometimes Robin would look into my face for a long time and give my dick the kindest caress before picking up her briefcase and going out the door. At night she cooked me large portions of food, with big bowls of rice and rich sauces, which, surprisingly, soothed my stomach rather than the reverse. And finally, after a few months, I felt much stronger, and so one sunny morning in the middle of the summer, on a sudden impulse, I looked for Rose's business card, and I called her number. Rose invited me over to her apartment on Apple Street, where she conducted a small design business right out of her home—she designed fantastically colored plates and cups—and so when I went over, there were a lot of cups and computers covering her bed, but we moved them quickly out of the way, and then we took off our clothes and sat on top of her bright green sheets. Her vagina looked just like the one in the picture, I rather blandly remarked—in other words, we had a little informal conversation, we exchanged a few thoughts—and soon we were fucking, it felt good, Rose came quickly and happily, and I sort of glowed with a kind of warmth as my orgasm seemed so painless and free. Right at its height, I suddenly felt something big and furry probing my asshole. I twisted around—and there was Blanche sitting quietly behind me, her whiskery face looking sheepish and humorous. Rose pulled Blanche towards her with a joyful smile, and it was totally clear that Rose had fallen in love with Blanche during the period of time in which they'd lived together. And Blanche had changed. Cuddled cozily against Rose's breasts, there was something so likable about her now. As she wiggled her paws around Rose's arms, I found that I too was now laughing with delight. And when Rose and I made love again, the unexpected way that Blanche managed to wind herself around our asses as our genitals bumped softly against each other, seemed to Rose like the funniest thing in the world. Afterwards, I stared at Rose as she drifted off into a little sleep, and then Blanche

walked slowly across the sheets and nuzzled against me.
I looked into her face, which was oddly beautiful. Her per-
sonality was so thoughtful now. She was amusing, gentle.
She'd become a friend.

(Music.)

Now, before we go on to the last part of our presentation,
I think we all may need a very brief snack of some kind.

*(The actors serve apples, hard-boiled eggs, nuts, chocolate,
etc. The music continues.)*

Part Three

The music continues. Eventually, strange images appear on the screen. Finally we see some film of Cerise walking in the country. Then, after a while, Cerise appears. She sits on the sofa for a while. Then she speaks to the audience. The film eventually fades out.

CERISE

I liked my life in my cabin in the woods. It's hard to say, but I might have liked it better than any life I'd ever lived before. The silence was beautiful—like a great ocean of whiteness in which I stretched and floated day after day. At night I heard pine needles touching in the wind, with the brook behind them—not bad, eh? All the same, after a while, I got awfully tired of the food that you could buy in the local shops, and I got tired of my own cooking, too, I have to admit. There was a little town not too far away, but it only had one restaurant—"Bill's"—and to be absolutely frank, Bill's wasn't the greatest. So I decided to rent a small apartment in that new part of the city that was sprawling out towards the north—what we now call "Pinville"—a soulless little district, undeniably, but very very quiet. There was an old woman who made vanilla pudding and sold it in a sort of barn-like space on the ground floor of my building, and people from all over the city started to come to buy this vanilla pudding, and one day I was in the pudding shop, and a beautiful woman came up to me and started speaking to me. She touched my arm, and she had a lovely touch, and my whole body relaxed when she touched me. She'd been in my house—she'd seen pictures of me there. I walked outside with her—it was a greasy, sweaty, hazy day—and we kept on walking, out by the banks of the river, until it was almost dark, sometimes talking, sometimes walking in silence. And so Robin and I became friends. Well—special friends. I felt—something—I was happy, I guess, when I was with her. The way she said words seemed so charming to me. And she had no moods—can you imagine that? She was always the same. Nothing disturbed her calm surface. No emotions at all, as far as I could tell.

HE

For the next several months, I went over to Rose's place on Apple Street almost every morning.

ROSE

I'd make some tuna fish salad for him, we'd eat, and then he and Blanche and I would race to the bedroom.

HE

Rose and I would take off our clothes, and then Rose and Blanche and I would crawl underneath the bright green sheets, and Rose would lead us through these ridiculous, hilarious games. In the afternoons, Blanche would go out the window to the fire escape and disappear to God knows where, and Rose would take a very long nap, and then at night I'd go home to Pushbroom Lane, where Robin kept me well informed about her friendship with Cerise.

ROBIN

(To him) Darling—I saw Cerise today. She gave me—a present.

HE

Really? What was it?

ROBIN

She gave me a beautiful pitcher.

HE

She did? That's amazing. What kind of a pitcher?

ROBIN

It's a beautiful glass water pitcher . . . *(Silence)*

HE

Hm . . . Things made of glass— *(Pause)* —can be sort of bad presents— *(Pause)* —in a way—because—when you break them, it seems like—bad luck . . .

ROBIN

Well, it's a beautiful pitcher. I'm certainly not going to break it. Why would—

HE

No, I just meant, why did she give you something you have to worry about?

ROBIN

I'm not going to worry about it. *(Pause)* And—I'm—I'm—I'm not going to break it.

(He is silent.)

HE

(To the audience) Robin broke the pitcher at the end of the summer. By October, things were going seriously wrong—and I don't mean only that the leaves started dropping off of the trees.

ROSE

Blanche became restless, nervous, unpredictable. She started wandering away for days at a time. Then she'd suddenly reappear, and a few days later she'd go off again.

HE

Rose was, unfortunately, much less fun when Blanche wasn't around. At first I'd found it so charming that Rose had a child's haircut and dressed like a child and was always barefoot, but eventually I began to notice that the only thing she really liked to do with me was to sit on her big white fluffy couch all day fully dressed and kiss. She was in a way like a dog who never gets tired of a particular game. But after so much kissing, I'd be almost desperate to be soothed inside her, and I noticed, as the months passed, that my visits to Apple Street became less and less frequent.

68

ROBIN

The nights sitting next to him on Pushbroom Lane were cold and grim. We spoke very little and never touched.

HE

I was over sixty, and as I sat next to Robin on those some-what painful nights, I was thinking about all the things I would have liked to do but realized now I would probably never do. Then Cerise asked Robin to go away on a trip.

CERISE

Robin and I went off on a boat to a sunny island. We stayed in a big hotel. For most of every day, I'd lie on top of my bed in the semi-darkness of my room, half awake and sweating. But a few times Robin and I went swimming in the nude. There was something "sexual" about that, somehow. God, I love that word. Admittedly, I looked at her private area once or twice. It was small, rather formal. The pleasure I'd once taken in sun and warm weather began to return. I did ask Robin if she wanted to come live with me, but she didn't reply.

ROBIN

(To him) Yes, I was happy, is that so intolerable?

HE

You have a right to happiness, certainly. And I have a right to feel any way I like about you and to behave in any way I like as well.

ROBIN

(To the audience) There was something thuggish in the way he said that. From then on, I was on my guard.

CERISE

(To the audience) After Robin and I came back from our trip, I used to go over to see her all the time. One day I dropped in unannounced. It turned out she'd suddenly gone away on business—but he was there.

HE

We sat on two sofas looking across at each other.

CERISE

I took off my shoes and socks and grinned idiotically, staring him in the face. The next week, I visited again. Sometimes we'd find ourselves kissing a bit, and then a few weeks later we started to fuck. The fact was, it was true: I liked to have his dick inside me—it gave me something to think about.

HE

Cerise talked constantly, obsessively about Robin. She was crazy about her.

CERISE

Relatively often, I'd meet Robin for lunch at some pleasant, sunny restaurant in the center of town, and we'd talk and laugh, and then I'd quietly stroll over to Pushbroom Lane.

HE

Cerise and I were making love all the time, and sometimes she'd leave her panties lying around, occasionally posed provocatively—near the toilet, for example. That began to get on Robin's nerves. One night Robin found Cerise's red brassiere rather nastily flung across a bowl of red flowers. When she saw the brassiere, she shuddered violently, and the next morning, she was unusually quiet as she went out the door. That night, she didn't come back, and no one knew where she'd gone, it seemed. Cerise was extraordinarily upset. She wrote Robin a letter in care of her office, and she gave the letter a title, "Letter To A Bird."

CERISE

"I only asked you, Robin, where you wanted to live—but flight, perhaps, was itself your answer. Is it always that way—in the world of birds? Is that the bird's awful, silent response—to everything? Flight?"

HE

Then Robin called Cerise on the telephone.

ROBIN'S VOICE

But why do you sound so terribly sad? What's wrong? It's as if you somehow think I was trying to hurt you . . .

CERISE

Yes—yes, that's what I think.

ROBIN'S VOICE

But my God—you've known nothing but love from me. Don't you realize that?

CERISE

Oh come on—please—I know that's true . . . And yet—

ROBIN'S VOICE

"And yet," she says. "And yet. And yet." I can't believe it.

CERISE

(To the audience) When I put down the phone, I felt a terrible pain in my stomach. Later in the day, I went out to do some shopping and met three different people in different shops who told me they were somehow feeling strangely unwell. And within a week everyone in the city was using this whole new vocabulary—"food problems," "problems with food." Everyone felt cold—everyone was shivering. Everyone suddenly seemed to agree that the water in the city—maybe even the *air*—could make it all feel worse, so most people who could do so were fleeing to the country. After a week of terribly painful vomiting, I took off once more to my cabin in the woods.

HE

For that whole freezing cold winter, I talked to almost no one except Dr. Gross. The strip clubs didn't open until four in the afternoon, so I'd wake up just in time to catch the first show at Spoons, a nice little place near the antiquities market. I'd masturbate there and have some breakfast. But one day one of the girls got horribly sick on stage. It was a rather lengthy, painful display, and so eventually I left, and when I stepped onto the street I bumped right into Rose. It had probably been a year since I'd last seen her. I almost didn't recognize her, she looked so different. She looked more grown up, she was dressed in black and white, with a purplish dark lipstick. She took me home to Apple Street, and Blanche greeted us at the door. Rose and I tried to make love, but she very quickly had to run to the bathroom to vomit, and when she came back, we hugged each other for a long time. And from then on, almost every afternoon, I'd go over to Apple Street, and Rose and I would sit next to each other in our pajamas in bed, reading magazines and taking turns vomiting in her rather cold bathroom, and Blanche would sit with us on the bed for hours at a time.

ROSE

Then one day Blanche went out, and she didn't come back. As more days passed, and she didn't return, I lost control of myself. I screamed, I cried. "Where is she? Where is she?" I repeated crazily as I sat in bed, compulsively painting dots on dark blue plates.

HE

I was sick anyway, so I couldn't stand the crying. I kept going out and running through the streets. Well, I'd never particularly liked Robin's husband, Mike, and he didn't like me, but one day I was out in the street, and I impulsively decided to throw myself on his mercy, so I went to see him, and after a brief discussion he gave me Robin's address. She was staying in a rather chic apartment building in a rather chic neighborhood near Mandrill Avenue. When I rang her bell, it was hardly past sunset, so I was surprised to find her totally out of it, as if she were incredibly drunk, but then I figured that she must have gotten hooked on one of those coyly shaped, cutely colored, very aggressive new painkillers that everyone seemed to be sucking on now. At first she refused to let me in the door, then she pulled me inside and gave me an enormous cocktail— *(To her)* —papers strewn in a disorderly fashion across the desk— Well, there was something depressing about seeing that, yes. I mean, they *were* my papers, the stupid book I was trying to write. And of course you should have told me that you already had that blue sweater that I kept on looking for all over town—I suppose you got it from Mike, or . . . And then, the water-colors?—the Paul Klee? Now, that was bad.

ROBIN

The Paul Klee?

HE

Well, you said you were going to buy it, as a present for Ed.

ROBIN

Yes, that's right . . .

HE

And the next day, when I asked you about it, you said you'd bought it.

ROBIN

Yes—yes?—

HE

But the night of the party, it wasn't there.

ROBIN

What the fuck? I don't know what I did with it. What the fuck?—I lost it. I lost it. I just—lost it . . .

HE

I don't believe you. I think you're lying. But *please*—I didn't come here to talk about that—I came here to talk about—something else.

ROBIN

Really? What?

HE

Oh, come on, Robin.

ROBIN

No, really. Really. What? *What?*

HE

I'm talking about what you took from us . . . Stealing. Stealing. You know, Robin—"against the law"? A *criminal* activity?

ROBIN

What are you saying? Is something missing? Or what in the world are you trying to say?

HE

I think you know what's missing, Robin.

ROBIN

I do not.

HE

Where is the cat? Where is Blanche?

ROBIN

What? You're not serious.

HE

Where—

ROBIN

You think I have something to do with *that*?

HE

Where is she?

ROBIN

I swear to God—

HE

(To the audience) At that precise moment, Blanche walked into the room and sat on the sofa. Then no one spoke for a long time. Finally she said:

ROBIN

All right—get out. Get out of my apartment.

HE

I'm taking Blanche.

ROBIN

Oh no you're not.

HE

(To the audience) I lunged towards Blanche. Robin slapped me in the face, she grabbed me and pushed me, I stumbled and fell, and then she picked up a large knife from the kitchen counter, ran back to the sofa, and slashed at Blanche with incredible strokes, ripping her body with almost impossible speed. Blood flowed over the sofa. One of Blanche's paws fell onto the rug. I wrestled with Robin, but Blanche was dead, there was nothing I could do . . . Robin ran into the bathroom and locked the door. I banged on the door with all my strength, then ran outside screaming, and I just kept on running. Just short of Apple Street, I stopped at a pharmacy and bought some sedatives, then I trudged in a ghastly state to Rose's apartment to tell her what had happened. It took her a very long time to grasp

what I was saying, then she became hysterical, and then sick. She finally agreed to take some of the capsules, and then she passed quickly into a deep sleep. Long after midnight, I went outside for a walk, and the gloomy streets led me slowly to Pushbroom Lane, but when I came in the door and tried to turn on the lights, they wouldn't turn on. The bulbs had been smashed. Slowly, in the darkness, I crept upstairs. I went into the bathroom, which was white with moonlight. Someone had pulverized the contents of the medicine chest, it seemed. My shoes were squelching through a thick cereal of pills, cough syrup, and broken glass. Then I heard a sort of moan, and I saw that Robin was lying on the bedroom floor. The curtains on all the windows were ripped, and there was a horrible smell. Urine dripped from the bed—from the blankets, the sheets. *(To Robin)* My God—what have you done?

ROBIN

(Extremely out of it) I tried to call you. No one answered.

HE

What's going on?

ROBIN

I don't know.

HE

What's going on?

ROBIN

Be careful with the sarcasm. I've still got the knife.

HE

(To the audience) She was curled into a corner of the dark bedroom with the knife pressed against her throat.

ROBIN

What's the matter? You seem frightened. What is it? What? Are you literally afraid to speak to me?

HE

I'm—

ROBIN

You poor thing—your life is awful!

HE

No—

ROBIN

What a bully you are. It's like that day last year. That was an awful day. I missed you—I *missed* you—I left work—I hurried home. I came to see you. I walked in the door—I mean, I simply walked in. That's all I did. And the response from you was, "What do you want from me?" Oh my God! I've learned—I've learned how brutal you are.

HE

Robin—please—

ROBIN

No—this is awful. You seem unhappy. *(Crying)*

HE

(To the audience) She reached out for me, held me, and cried for a long time, caressing me sweetly as we lay on the floor, the knife beside us. I felt an impulse to get her out of my house. "Do you want to go get something to eat?" I asked. "Yes, yes." So we walked down the street to the neighborhood café where so many years before we'd often found ourselves an early breakfast. But when we got to the café, we had a surprise: there was a sign in the window— the place was closed. Yes, our neighborhood café, always intelligently run, had come to a logical business decision which most other similar establishments ended up making just a month or two later. And when I look back on the two of us standing there, what's surprising is that the whole situation was so new at that time, and so poorly understood, that I didn't have the faintest idea that what was going on with Robin had nothing to do with those new painkillers. A few weeks later, the words "unusual behavior" would be constantly on the lips of every single person fortunate enough not to be behaving unusually themselves—and the phrase "unusual behavior, followed by a short illness and death" would suddenly be a formula heard much more frequently than "sun, followed by clouds and late-afternoon showers." Anyway, the night with Robin ended, I thought, in an unexpected way. We went back to the house, where she used both her hands in an out-of-it but still rather purposeful manner to remove my trousers and force my member inside her. And then she dressed quickly and asked me to watch her—and even to help her—as she went through different closets and found piles of old makeup, her own and Cerise's, which, despite my attempts to assist her, she

applied with a definite awkwardness, as her coordination
was obviously not quite what it should have been. In any
event, there was no amount of makeup which could have
prevented her face from conveying the message that she was
both sick and insane, although she did manage to coax her
skin into giving off a sort of metallic sheen which was odd
and fascinating and in a way alluring, one had to admit. And
then she asked me to bring her over to Mike's, where in fact
she remained for several weeks, until he and then she came to
the typical end of life which everyone now knew they would
eventually reach, the moment when the vomiting didn't stop.

ROBIN

He sat close to me on the long taxi ride to Mike's across
the glamorous city, and when Mike came out onto the very
dark street in a bathrobe, looking thin but manly, he held
Mike's arm for a moment before getting back into the taxi
and speeding away.

HE

From Mike's place, I went back to Apple Street, and I awakened Rose, and took her for a visit to Dr. Gross. And then
I called Cerise in the country and asked her to do a great
favor for me. I asked her if she'd be willing to take in this
sweet girlfriend of mine, because Gross felt quite certain
that some time in the country would be all that would be
needed to bring Rose back to a state of moderate health or
at the very least to save her life for a while. Cerise sounded
tired, but she quickly agreed, and so Rose departed, and
I soon learned from Cerise that it was going well. Cerise
really liked Rose. She found her clever and funny, and they
shared a feeling for all sorts of animals.

CERISE

Rose was adorable. It all was easy, even though the two of us were living in a cabin built for one. The months passed quietly. Every now and then, I'd go stay with Ben for a week or two, enjoy the luxury of his big expensive bed, see Dr. Gross, take some walks through the old parts of the city. Sometimes, at night, while I was urinating on him—urine filling up his navel as if it were a little cup, then spilling everywhere—I would look out the window and off into the darkness of sky and cloud, and I would lower my ass, sputtering a bit, and sit on top of him, as he'd be growling nastily into the blackness, and I'd blow a kiss towards him in an affectionate way, even though there was very little left that was likable about him. And then sometimes he'd lean against the pillows, and we'd sit beside each other, looking out the window, his monstrous paw curled around me.

But finally the trips into the city became too hard to do. It was a difficult journey, and I wasn't well. So, after a couple of years, in the end it was Rose who went back down to take care of Ben as he proceeded towards death.

On that sunny island we'd gone to several years before, Robin had given me Granville's book to read. There were no real surprises in it for me, but when I showed it to Rose and explained it a bit, she was quite upset.

ROSE

Eventually, in the progression of our peculiar illness, most people reached a point at which they just couldn't eat potatoes. Cerise had passed that point long ago, and so one day she brought me over to her potato bin and said, "Look— isn't this awful? They're going to waste. You have to eat them." "But those are your potatoes!" I said, alarmed, thinking that maybe she'd go back to them one day. "No. Please," she said. So I put almost all the potatoes into a big pot, and I boiled them all up, and then, with Cerise just outside working in the garden, I put the potatoes into a bowl with butter and salt and pepper, and I just ate and ate—you know, crying every once in a while, obviously, but still enjoying them more than I can tell you. And that was the last time I ever ate potatoes.

Cerise needed me to take care of Ben, but the pain of leaving her was more terrible than anything I'd ever felt. The last days before I went down to the city, I begged to stay with her, I pleaded, but she'd made up her mind.

The city was dirtier now—black with dirt. And as for Ben—well, you know, Ben was bitter. He'd expected more from life, he'd wanted more, so his disposition was by this time—mm—hideously atrocious—does that convey my point?—and his normal way of speaking, if he spoke at all, was a sort of sarcastic snarl, ugly and mean. So living on Pushbroom Lane couldn't be described as literally fun, quite apart from the fact that I was a servant, really, which was quite hard work. But I felt awfully fortunate compared to the people I saw lying down on the sidewalks and pressing their faces against the buildings.

For most of every day, Ben stayed in bed, dozing. I'd sit beside him with a pad of paper and my box of paints and paint nighttime scenes of people who lived on the shore of a lake and the extraordinary things that happened to them. Cerise wrote me letters that were painful to read, about the sickness and death of the animals who lived near her in the woods. Occasionally in these letters she seemed to slip into a sort of delirium in which she wrote about her past—all sorts of things I could barely understand.

(Rose activates the mechanical device, and we see Cerise in another bit of film. She wears very strange makeup, and her face is partly transformed.)

CERISE

"And around nine in the evening, we'd get up from our naps, and we'd take off our pajamas, put on our little bells, and it would be time for dinner—banquets, parties, dancing, music. And sometimes we'd wear costumes or elaborate disguises, sometimes we'd invite other animals over, or men, people, we'd play cards, we'd gamble, put on plays, do magic shows. And that was how we lived."

ROSE

And here's another one.

(Rose activates another bit of film, in which Cerise's face is completely transformed.)

CERISE

"Every Wednesday I'd get up very very early, stick my face into a bowl full of coffee, put on my red ribbon, and then go into a little conference room and meet my advisors. They'd present me with a list of the problems of the day, we'd discuss things a bit, I'd make some decisions, and within less than two hours I'd be back in my pajamas and back in my bed. And then I'd always fall into a particularly nice sleep, and I'd start the day again at noon or so, just when everyone else was getting up. Yawn, stretch, peek at the sun on the grass outside the curtains, and then go down to the dining room and have some breakfast. Yes, you guessed it— mice again! Ha ha ha— *(She laughs merrily)* Those poor little mice! Ha ha ha ha. —Oh come on, it's funny! Those poor little mice . . . Of course you have to understand that over the centuries we all took turns putting on a bright red ribbon and deciding things. Every decade or so it would be the next cat's turn, so each of us knew that if we made terrible decisions, they'd probably be corrected later."

(The film flickers out.)

ROSE

Cerise's last letter was very short. It simply said, "Coming in to see Gross. Dinner Thursday?" And that was the last I heard.

(Then Cerise speaks to the audience.)

CERISE

(To the audience) We're telling the story of Ben, and we've come to the end of the story, the last moments.

ROBIN

(To the audience) The scale of his crimes meant that he deserved the most severe punishment—death. The funny thing was that this was the very same punishment given to people who'd hardly done anything wrong at all. Perhaps he should have been made to die in agony, as those whose deaths he had caused had died in agony. But there'd been much too much agony on earth already.

ROSE

(To the audience) His body would not be tormented. But before entering the realm of death, he'd be forced to give up

some of the false beliefs that had served as his view of himself and the world. First he'd have to learn about something humorous, then about something unbearable and bad.

CERISE

(To the audience) Often, in their last moments on earth, people figure things out. They put two and two together. They realize that the things they only dimly suspected were actually true after all.

(Ben goes to the lectern and speaks to the audience.)

HE

I don't know—I keep having the feeling that my memoirs are somehow a bit out of date . . . *(He throws the memoir in the waste basket and finishes drinking the bottle of liquid)* Mm . . . At any rate, following the instructions on the invitation I'd received at my breakfast table, I did drive myself out late yesterday afternoon to this sort of suburban area that I'd rarely visited. I arrived at a large house, and when Blanche opened the front door, I saw that indeed she was a woman now—not any longer the cat who had died on Robin's sofa—but in a way she really hadn't changed that much—she still seemed like Blanche. She brought me through the house, and we sat on a patio from which we could look down onto a large lawn, filled with a great many guests, some of whom she described to me in the apparently rather conventionally confiding manner of a kindly, middle-aged, bourgeois hostess. Her skin was pale, like the white-washed walls of the house, and she obviously had a few scars on her face, a few odd slashes, well concealed by makeup, but of course she was pretty, very very pretty, with

85

tiny teeth, and a pretty pink tongue, and pink lipstick—but then I noticed something quite surprising, which was that the dress she was wearing, which I found awfully nice, was actually a dress I'd once bought for Cerise. And as that began sinking in on me, I found myself staring at Blanche's neck, where a large pink wound was almost covered up by a red ribbon, decorated with bells.

CERISE

And that was when he realized that a very funny joke had been played on him for most of his adult life.

HE

Yes, it was obviously funny that the cat I'd played with in Rose's bed had been Cerise, and the cat I hadn't liked on Pushbroom Lane had been Cerise, and the white cat in the palace, whom I'd loved and who had truly known me, had been Cerise, too.

ROSE

He knew it was funny. He realized it was funny. But he also began to feel a bit faint. He tried to stand up. He leaned against the wall. But before he could pass out, Blanche took him by the arm and led him down to the lawn below.

HE

In the middle of the lawn there was a very nice pool, and there were some children—were they hers?—who were swimming in it, and so Blanche brought me over to a shady spot where we could watch the children, and there were some lawn chairs there, and so we sat down, and we continued our chat. We talked about people we'd known, whatever, and then after a while someone brought me some tea, along with a plate of delicious cold chicken, which I ate for a while and then set down on the grass, and that was when Blanche mentioned the album of photographs of her recent life which she took out of a bag and seemed eager to show me. *(Cerise gives him the album. Music as he opens it)* But when I opened the album with a polite smile, I saw page after page of sort of dark city sidewalks, filled with the curled-up bodies of old people, children, women, men, and there were black landscapes, covered with dead animals, animals of every kind, and pictures of the wilderness, with dead cats lying in piles under enormous trees, with green ribbons and bells falling across them, and I understood that the people and the animals were the ones I'd killed. And then Blanche and I sat there in silence for a long time.

ROBIN

(To the audience) Each one of us reaches death by a separate path, but I must say, the last part of the journey is really shocking. I mean, it covers an awful lot of ground awfully fast and sort of takes your breath away. Anyway, I'm sure you all have lots of opinions about death and how it ought to be organized and managed. But one thing I know you'll like about it is that after death you can have some awfully interesting conversations. After death, the murderer and his victim can sit down together and have a perfectly nice talk, because the murderer can't murder anymore, and the victim can't be murdered anymore. All the suffering is over. I mean, after death a person becomes like a rock or a table, a chair or a star—not alive and unable to suffer.

ROSE

(To the audience) And yet the murder that happened did happen, and the suffering that happened did happen, and that can never be erased.

HE

As we sat there in the shade, it was getting late, and Blanche and I both began to feel chilly, but high above us the sky was still blue, and parts of the lawn were still sparkling with sun. Blanche started speaking to me amusingly again about this and that, and against the background of all the usual murmuring of suburban insects and the sounds of the children splashing in the pool, her voice seemed so melodious and gentle that at a certain point tears began to fall out of my eyes, just the way they had at that puppet show. But then—when the sun didn't set, and the party didn't end, and Blanche quietly said for a second time some of the very same things she'd said before, well, of course I realized what was happening, and I saw that this time there was absolutely nothing I could do about it, and then I felt the chicken moving around in my throat, and I knew I was about to get very sick. Blanche walked me to the door of a bathroom in the house whose wallpaper portrayed expressionless soldiers from some distant time. And then I closed the bathroom door, and I began to vomit. And it got pretty painful. But then Blanche decided to take pity on me.

She knocked on the door, led me out of the bathroom, and explained that there was after all a somewhat nicer way out, a sort of back door that could be used—I mean, it was all rather special, and most people didn't know about it, but it had always been my lot to be lucky, and there didn't seem to be any reason why that should stop now, particularly.

So we went outside again, and Blanche pointed the way to an enormous meadow, filled with buttercups, across which one could walk until one pleasantly fell asleep, with no vomiting at all.

CERISE

We looked at the meadow, and I held him close to me for a brief moment, and then I sent him on his way.

HE

Well, as you might have guessed, it was just the time of day in which the direct sun on one's face was totally agreeable and not at all too hot, and, sure enough, by the time I was halfway across the meadow I desperately wanted to lie down and fall asleep.

So I found a very pleasant mossy spot, and I curled up pleasantly in a comfortable position, and—you know—what can I say?—I mean, please don't be envious—I have to admit, it felt quite nice.

(The lights grow very cold before they go out. The three women sit together talking. Ben sits by himself.)

END

Author's Note

Let's be frank—I've taken a few elements of this play from the story "The White Cat" by Madame d'Aulnoy (1650/51–1705). This story can be found in Andrew Lang's *The Blue Fairy Book* (first published by Longmans, Green, and Co, 1889; republished by Dover Publications, 1965). John Ashbery's translation appears in Marina Warner's *Wonder Tales* (Farrar, Straus and Giroux, 1996).